TRAPPED IN TIME

"Time travel can be dangerous," I told her.

My cousin, Ashley, rolled her eyes.

"All right, James. Tell me how dangerous."

I figured I'd tell it to her straight. "We have no idea where we might end up."

"So?"

"So we could easily pop up in the middle of a rock! Or at the bottom of an ocean. Or who knows where!" I explained.

"All right, James." She sighed. "I think I get the idea. But maybe we'd pop up safe and sound back at Paramount's Kings Island. Right where we started from. Or in your mom's kitchen, just as she's taking one of her chocolate pies out of the oven."

Ashley's blue eyes sparkled. "Don't you think it's worth the risk, James? I say we go for it!"

She reached for one of the knobs in the time machine.

Also by R. L. Stine

The Beast

Available from MINSTREL Books

THE
BEAST® 2

A Parachute Press Book

A MINSTREL® BOOK

PUBLISHED BY POCKET BOOKS

New York   London   Toronto   Sydney   Tokyo   Singapore

This book is a work of fiction. Names, characters, places, and incidents are products of the author's imagination or are used fictitiously. Any resemblance to actual events or locales or persons, living or dead, is entirely coincidental.

A MINSTREL PAPERBACK *ORIGINAL*

A Minstrel Book published by
POCKET BOOKS, a division of Simon & Schuster Inc.
1230 Avenue of the Americas, New York, NY 10020

Copyright © 1995 by Parachute Press, Inc.

ISBN: 0-671-52951-X

First Minstrel Books printing June 1995

10 9 8 7 6 5 4 3 2 1

THE BEAST® is a registered trademark of Paramount Parks Inc. All rights reserved.

A MINSTREL BOOK and colophon are registered trademarks of Simon & Schuster Inc.

Cover art by Broeck Steadman

Printed in the U.S.A.

1

The car clattered to a stop on the wooden tracks. I let my breath out in a long, satisfied *whoosh*.

Then I turned to my cousin, Ashley Franks. "What did I tell you?" I croaked.

My throat was raw from screaming and laughing nonstop for the last four minutes.

Grinning, she unglued her hands from the safety bar. "You're right, James. That was superb!" she exclaimed.

Ashley and I hadn't been to Paramount's Kings Island together in almost a year. We were making up for it fast. Already we had ridden The Beast three times.

1

This last time we did something a little different. We closed our eyes going down the steepest hill.

It sounds easy, but it isn't. With your eyes squeezed shut while the car pitches straight down the tracks, it feels as if the world has dropped out from under you. And you're falling through the air. Just falling.

I grinned and pointed to Ashley's hair. It was standing up around her head. Sort of like a cartoon character that's free-falling off a cliff.

Laughing, she reached up to smooth it down. The Beast did that. Snarled your hair. Scrambled your insides, too.

It's the longest, scariest wooden coaster there is.

We climbed out of the car. My legs felt rubbery on the concrete platform. Everybody was talking about how great the ride was as they staggered dizzily toward the exit ramp.

As I weaved along, Ashley darted in front of me.

"Let's do it again, James." Her eyes sparkled mischievously as she danced along backward in front of me.

I turned on the ramp to stare up at the enormous roller coaster. It loomed big and black against the purple night sky.

Floodlights beamed down from the massive wooden scaffolding. They outlined the swirling, swooping, diving, soaring shape of The Beast.

I shivered.

People said that a ghost haunted The Beast at night.

Of course, people only make up that story to scare themselves. People love to scare themselves.

But deep down, they didn't really believe there was a ghost. It was just a story, right?

Well, my cousin and I knew differently.

Not that you could tell from the way Ashley was bubbling over tonight. She was all eager and excited to get back on The Beast.

I guess you could say that Ashley is the adventurous type—at least until she gets caught up in a for-real adventure. Then she sometimes wimps out.

Me, on the other hand, I don't exactly invite adventure. But when it comes my way, I'm pretty excited by it.

"It's getting late. . . ." I told her.

"Come on, James." She slapped me on the back.

I winced. "I'm tired," I complained.

I glanced at my watch. "Almost time for the park to close."

"Come on, James," she wheedled me. "One more time won't hurt. What's the matter? Full moon got you scared?"

I shrugged and looked up. The big orange moon was not quite full.

I heaved a sigh. "Okay, one more time." I held up a single finger.

"Yes!" Ashley exploded and started dancing me around in a circle.

"But first," I added, removing myself from her clutches, "I've got to go to the snack bar. I need an energy boost, big-time."

Ashley punched me on the arm. "Go for it."

She spun me around and shoved me in the direction of the snack bar. "Go reenergize. But hurry. I think they're starting to load the cars."

Ashley trotted over to the end of the line, her shiny pink clogs clip-clopping.

I hurried to the snack bar. Luckily, there was

only one kid ahead of me in line. Unluckily, he was moving in slow motion.

Staring at the green Day-Glo brontosaurus on the back of his T-shirt, I tried to burn two holes in his back so he'd hurry up. I mean, how long could it take to pick out a snack?

I glanced back. The line feeding into The Beast was beginning to move.

Ashley stamped her clogs and waved at me. I read her lips.

Hurry up!

I shrugged helplessly. I wasn't about to brave The Beast again without my Karamel Kreemies.

Karamel Kreemies is my favorite candy this summer. Last summer I liked Marshmallow Bombs. But for some reason, the company stopped making them.

So I've switched to Karamel Kreemies in a big way. Just as the commercial says, "if I don't get my Kreemies, I get the screamies."

Bronto-boy ahead of me was trying to decide between the Mango Mango Munchies and the Frootie-Toot-Toots. Personally, I like the Mango Mango Munchies better. The flavor lasts twice as long.

Two girls got in line behind me. One was tall

with a long brown braid. The other was short with punkish red hair. They were a little older than me and wore red checked shorts and identical short white T-shirts. Their socks and sneakers matched, too.

Why is it that girlfriends sometimes think it's so cool to dress exactly alike? Do they think people will mistake them for twins? These two couldn't even pass for distant cousins.

"Come on, Tiffany, I bet it's not that scary," the short one was telling her friend.

"Bet it is," Tiffany insisted.

Tiffany turned to size up The Beast. From where we stood, it was almost completely hidden by thick, dark woods.

You could hear it, though—the rattle of the wheels on the wooden tracks, the high-pitched squeals of the people in the cars. The screams rose and fell at the same time, like one great big shrill scream.

An amazing sound.

I guess that's why some people like to call it a scream machine.

The short one jerked her chin at me. "Why don't you ask him, Tiff. He just got off The Beast."

"Really?" Tiffany turned to stare at me as if I'd just returned from a trip to the moon.

I nodded modestly.

"Is it as scary as everybody says?" Tiffany asked eagerly.

I pretended to think about it. "Yeah. It's terrifying," I informed her.

Tiffany's eyes grew wider still, and she nudged her friend. "What did I tell you? No way are you getting me on that monster."

I sighed and smiled sadly. "Why come here if you don't want to be terrified? It's fun!"

I turned away from Tiffany and her friend to find that Slo-mo Day-Glo bronto-boy was still at it. Ashley was now signaling to me with frantic little jumping jacks as the line inched closer to the gate.

I finally tapped the kid on the shoulder. "Go for the Mango Mango Munchies," I told him. I *really* had the screamies now.

The kid turned, gnawing his lip uncertainly. His cheeks were sticky and pink from cotton candy.

"You really think so?" he asked.

"Trust me," I insisted.

I guess the kid knew an expert when he

heard one, because he put down the Frootie-Toot-Toots and paid for the Munchies. Plus five other pieces of candy.

And I thought *I* had it bad.

I scanned the rows of candy for the familiar screaming pink-and-purple roll. The jingle from the TV ad ran through my head: *"Kara-mel Kreemie, smooth and dreamie!"*

"Got them!" I grabbed the roll and almost threw the money at the lady behind the counter.

I tore back just in time to catch the tail end of the line being swallowed up by the gates.

I hurried up the ramp and onto the platform, scanning the cars for my cousin.

When I saw her, I stopped short and gasped.

I couldn't believe what I was seeing.

2

My cousin Ashley was sitting in the very first seat of the very first car.

She was grinning, looking extremely pleased with herself.

Everybody wanted to sit in those seats.

I mean, they were absolutely the best. Sitting in those seats, you could feel every twist and turn, every climb and swoop, ultra-magnified. Nothing stood between you and the terror.

And yet, my cousin had been practically the last in line. How had she managed to get the very best seats on the ride?

"Smooth move," I congratulated her.

Her blue eyes twinkled. "The kids who were

sitting here before chickened out at the last minute," she explained. She patted the seat next to her.

I nodded, impressed.

"Especially," she added smugly, "after I told them that the first car is haunted."

A creepy feeling made me shiver.

"Well, it's true, isn't it?" she asked.

I didn't answer. Instead, I jumped in just before the safety bar slammed down.

"What took you so long?" she demanded as I got settled. "I was afraid you wouldn't make it."

"It's a bnfnff nnnewry."

She leaned in toward me. "What?" she asked.

I guess I wasn't speaking very clearly. My teeth were glued together with gooey caramel. I swallowed.

"It's a long story," I repeated, then popped a second Kreemie in my mouth and chewed.

The incredibly sticky sweetness filled my mouth and slid down my throat like syrup.

Sugar heaven.

Smooth and dreamie.

But I was being rude.

"Want one?" I held out the roll to my cousin.

She shook her head and flashed me a mouth

full of braces. They were the new kind that came in bright colors rather than just plain metal. Hers were pink and purple.

It was sort of unfair. I mean, I couldn't even call her tinsel-teeth.

"I keep forgetting you have braces now," I told her.

She rolled her eyes. "How could anyone forget? I certainly can't. I can't eat candy or apples or corn on the cob or any of my favorite foods. I hate them."

Ashley is not too happy about the braces. Even though they're the new, cool kind, I think they embarrass her. She tries not to smile or laugh as much as she used to, but she pretty much can't help herself. She happens to be the laughing, smiling type.

I tell her she looks okay, braces and all, even though she doesn't believe me.

My cousin and I don't look at all alike. She's blond, blue-eyed, freckled, and peppy. I'm dark, brown-eyed and serious. At least that's how I come across.

Deep down, I think I've got a pretty good sense of humor. And I don't have braces. Or a single cavity in my head.

My mother says it's a minor miracle, considering how much candy I eat. I guess I'm just lucky.

I popped one more Karamel Kreemie into my mouth while I still had a chance and jammed the roll into the pocket of my jean shorts.

I felt a gentle tug as the car started to move forward.

"Here we go!" I heard the redheaded girl in the car behind us tell her boyfriend. The boyfriend sort of whimpered.

Ashley and I exchanged grins as the car began to pick up speed. Our heads thudded back against the headrests as we began to climb the first and steepest of the three hills. Higher and higher we crawled up the creaky wooden platform.

I took my eyes from the track long enough to shoot a glance at Ashley. She was staring wide-eyed at the top of the hill. It seemed to drop off into space. The car slowed to a standstill.

We teetered at the tip-top for a heart-stopping instant.

Far, far below us the dark treetops danced. As the cool wind whipped our hair and clothes,

I felt a sudden surge of happiness. Then we swooped straight down.

"Whoop!"

Down, down the car clattered.

My cousin flung up her arms, opened her mouth wide, and shrieked.

Down, down we dipped into the whirling, churning sea of trees.

We were hurtling through a jumble of lights and shadows and terrified screams.

I gripped the bar, arms stiff, screaming my head off.

Each time I ride The Beast, I tell myself this time I'll get through the ride without screaming.

Then I realize, halfway down the first hill, that screaming is what it's all about. And I open my mouth and out it comes. It feels great.

We whirled into an underground tunnel, the blackness billowing around us, swallowing us totally.

"Whooooooaaaa!" I heard Ashley cry.

Just as suddenly, we broke out of the tunnel, and zoomed around a sharp bend. Ashley grabbed my arm.

"Ooomph!"

Her long blond hair streamed into my eyes,

blinding me. I reached up to brush it away just as we zipped the other way.

She was laughing, shouting something about *"my favorite part, James!"*

Before I could reply, we tipped backward with a bump and started climbing another hill.

Then down we roared, stomachs churning, into the deep, dark valley. The wind pounded my cheeks and stung my eyes.

Bright lights rippled over me.

The car jolted level, whipping us into a tunnel so dark, I didn't know where I stopped and it began. It was like hurtling through deep space.

Out of the tunnel, we exploded in a burst of blinding bright light.

I panted, gasping for breath as the car scaled a hill, up and up toward that big orange moon. Then down again, tossed topsy-turvy through a tunnel.

And then we slowed.

My face felt chapped, almost wind-burned. Every tooth in my head tingled.

The car clattered to a stop on the wooden tracks.

I sat completely still with my eyes closed.

You know the way you feel after a day of swimming in the ocean surf? You lie in bed and you can still feel the waves tossing you every which way?

Well, there's a moment, right after the ride ends when, if you just sit there, with your eyes closed, you can relive every twist and turn, every climb and drop of the three-minute-and-forty-second ride.

I opened my eyes and exhaled.

"Great idea, Ashley. I'm glad you suggested it!" I exclaimed as I turned to my cousin.

I couldn't believe it.

This couldn't be happening.

Not again!

I shook my head and blinked. But it didn't change a thing.

The seat beside me where my cousin Ashley had been sitting seconds ago was empty.

Ashley was gone!

3

My heart was hammering in my chest.

Where was Ashley?

I put my hand over my heart to try and slow it. I needed to be calm. I needed to think clearly. I took deep breaths. Slower, slower.

I remembered Ashley beside me. I remembered her flinging her arms up going down that first hill.

I remembered her hair flying in my face.

And her screaming. My right ear was practically deaf from the sound of her shrill, sharp screaming.

Was there a point when her screaming stopped?

Had she had fallen out as we hurtled through one of the tunnels?

Impossible.

She couldn't fall out of the car with the safety bar down.

I felt the seat. It was still warm from her body. Could she have slipped out quickly just as the ride ended, before I opened my eyes?

If she was playing one of her cute tricks on me, I was going to kill her.

Well, maybe not kill her exactly. But seriously pound her, for sure.

I lifted the safety bar and climbed out of the car. I elbowed my way through the crowd up to the man in the blue uniform.

"Did you see a girl with blond hair and white shorts get off the ride?" I asked. My voice came out sounding pip-squeaky.

"Son," he replied sadly, "do you have any idea how many blond girls in white shorts I see here every day?"

I didn't think he expected an answer to that question, so I didn't give him one.

"She might have gotten off the ride early," I suggested hopefully. "Before it slowed down?"

He shook his head. "Not while I'm on duty!

The safety bar is locked until the car comes to a complete halt."

I glanced back into the cars, measuring with my eyes the distance between the bar and the seat.

"My cousin is pretty skinny," I explained. "She might have slipped out, even with the bar down."

"Impossible," the man said flatly. "Check down by the exit gate, why don't you?"

I nodded gloomily.

"Or check at the message center," he continued, pointing out over the heads of the exiting crowd. "Better make it snappy, though. The park's closing soon."

My eyes followed the direction of his finger to the tall replica of the Eiffel Tower that stands at the center of the park.

I nodded numbly and staggered down the ramp.

Ashley wasn't at the exit gate. She wasn't standing anywhere near it.

Might as well head for the message center near the tower.

But why was I even bothering?

There was no way she could have gotten off

the ride and gone over to the message center in time to leave me a message. I mean, why would she do a thing like that?

Besides, what sort of message would it be, anyway?

Dear James, I've disappeared into thin air. Just try and find me. Your Cousin Ashley.

My anger started boiling up again. My face felt hot. My hands were clenched in the pockets of my denim shorts.

I made my way past the Vortex. The Vortex is a giant steel roller coaster that turns you upside down and every which way. We'd ridden it before lunch, while our stomachs were still pretty empty.

Ever since we first saw it, Ashley and I have wondered what it would be like to sneak underneath the Vortex and collect all the loose change that must fly out of people's pockets when the coaster spins them upside down.

Maybe Ashley was underneath the Vortex right now, grubbing around on her hands and knees for loose change.

Maybe not.

I passed the old-time fifties café where they

serve burgers and shakes. A woman was pulling down the shutter.

I trotted over to the café, where a man was sponging off tables.

"Did a girl with long blond hair and pink clogs happen to grab a quick burger just now?" I asked breathlessly. "She likes her burgers plain. No ketchup or anything."

The man with the sponge straightened up. "Kitchen is closed for the night. She didn't stop here," he said.

I continued on. People streamed past me, tired and happy, heading for the parking lot. I searched among them for Ashley, my chest tightening by the second.

The park was about to close. And my cousin was nowhere in sight.

What was I supposed to do? Leave without her?

I passed the basketball game booth, its lights out, its hoops still and empty.

Only this afternoon Ashley had bet me five dollars I couldn't sink eight free throws in a row. Ashley lost.

I reached into my pocket and felt the wilted five-dollar bill I had won from her.

"Ashley!" I yelled, turning in a tight circle and scanning the crowd. "I'll give you back your five dollars if you show your face . . . right now!"

A few strangers flashed me funny looks. But no Ashley popped up among them to claim her five dollars.

I jogged along, checking to the left and right, scanning the darkened game booths, souvenir stands, and snack bars. Was she hiding in the shadows, peering out at me? Was she having a good laugh?

How could she put me through this? Did she actually think it was funny?

It wasn't funny.

"Ladies and gentlemen," a woman's voice crackled over the loudspeaker system, "Paramount's Kings Island is now closing. Please make your way to the exits and have a nice night."

I was most definitely *not* having a nice night.

I felt myself being pushed along with the crowd as it streamed toward the Eiffel Tower, and the gates beyond. Then I froze and let the crowd flow around me.

I turned slowly and looked back in the direction of The Beast.

Maybe I was going the wrong way.

Maybe she had never really left The Beast.

Maybe if I went back right now, I would find her.

Ashley would be waiting for me on the darkened platform, hugging herself, her big blue eyes wide and scared.

Then again, maybe she was waiting for me at the gate, arms crossed, tapping her foot, angry because *I* had wandered off.

I stood on the path and looked one way, then the other.

I didn't know which way to go, backward or forward.

I didn't know whether to be angry or scared.

One thing I did know.

I wasn't leaving this park tonight. No way.

Not without my cousin.

4

I had to stay in the park after the gates were closed and locked. Where could I hide? At closing time the place was crawling with security guards in blue suits.

I whipped around and raced back along International Street, past the still fountains, back into the heart of the park.

The air had grown damp and the orange moon was now shrouded in a thick, green mist.

I felt cold. Maybe it was the sudden darkness. The emptiness. The quiet.

Only minutes ago the park had been brightly lit and crowded. The fountains had been gushing, and cheerful music had blared over the loudspeakers.

Now the lights were dim. The fountains were turned off. The loudspeakers silent. As I jogged along, the tiny lights in the soles of my sneakers blinked, first one, then the other, like a signal.

An SOS signal.

But there was no one here to help me. If I told one of the guards, he'd make me go to the office.

The restaurants, the stores, the booths—everything was closed and padlocked and dark. The only sound I heard was the breeze riffling the treetops.

I stopped and stared down into a reflecting pool. It shimmered like black glass. My face stared up at me, pinched and worried.

I couldn't believe this was happening. A sick, panicky feeling squeezed my throat.

My head jerked up at a sudden noise.

Someone was coming from the direction of the games alley. I ran and ducked behind a wastebasket next to a lemonade stand.

The wastebasket smelled like lemons. My nose twitched.

Two security guards strolled past, the beams of their flashlights sweeping the path. They paused in front of the stand.

24

My stomach flip-flopped. My nose twitched again. I felt a sneeze tickling at the back of my throat. Don't tell me I had developed a sudden allergy to lemons!

They played their flashlight beams across the bushes behind me and came to rest on the wastebasket. I curled myself into a tiny ball and pinched my nose to stifle a sneeze.

"Wish I'd bet on that game," one of them said to the other. "I'd be a rich man today."

"You and me both," the other replied. "I could use a glass of lemonade right about now."

"A cup of hot tea would be more like it," his partner replied. "I think we're in for some rain tonight."

The flashlight beam swept away from me as the guards resumed their patrol.

I let out my breath in a *whoosh* of relief. I sneezed quickly three times.

I felt awful.

I couldn't believe I was hiding from the guards again. I couldn't believe any of this was happening again.

But it was.

Last summer Ashley and I were locked in the park after it closed. On a dare I went along with my cousin's crazy plan to spend the night in the park.

At the foot of The Beast we had met an old bearded man in overalls who tested the cars at night. His name was P. D. Walters.

P.D. had told us all about Firelight Park, the amusement park that had once stood on the same spot as Paramount's Kings Island. Sixty years ago it had been destroyed by a tornado. Hundreds of people were killed. It was a tragic story.

Then P.D. offered to let us have a ride on The Beast through the swirling nighttime fog.

The ride had been awesome.

There had been only one problem.

We traveled into the past.

Sixty years into the past.

To Firelight Park.

We met a boy named Paul. He was showing us a great time until a newspaper blew by. The date on the newspaper was the day the tornado was due to hit.

Nobody believed us when we tried to warn them. It was only as the tornado was practically on top of us that we made an amazing discovery. Our young friend Paul and P. D.

Walters, were the exact same people, from two different times.

Luckily for us, we found The Beast and jumped on just in time. We escaped the tornado and went tearing back to the present.

But we had failed to get Paul to come along with us.

I'll never forget.

As we were leaving the park that night, we spied Paul's name, among many others, engraved on a memorial plaque near the front gate.

Then we knew two things.

Our friend Paul had not survived the tornado.

And P.D., the old man in the overalls, wasn't really a special nighttime worker of the amusement park.

P.D. was a ghost. The ghost of young Paul, who died in flames so many years ago.

The stories people told were true.

The Beast really was haunted.

I could barely stand to think about it. But I had a terrible feeling Ashley wasn't just lost somewhere in the park.

Ashley was lost in time!

5

I knelt there behind the trash can, hugging my-self to keep warm. A fine rain had begun to sift down from the low mist hanging overhead.

Just my luck. And me without so much as a windbreaker to keep me dry.

I pulled up the damp collar of my maroon-and-white striped soccer jersey.

I've wondered a lot about time travel since that night last summer.

Did The Beast itself send us roaring back-ward into the past? Or did P.D. flick the switches that sent us back?

In the last year I've read every book on the subject of time travel I could get my hands on.

Some of them are hard to understand. Most are pretty fascinating.

I've read H. G. Wells's *The Time Machine.* Plus dozens of fantasy and science fiction stories.

I've also rented every movie about time travel ever made.

What I've learned is that there are lots of different ways to travel through time. All kinds of time machines and ways to send yourself back and forth.

And somehow last summer when we were riding The Beast, we were sucked back sixty years in time to Firelight Park. I don't know how or why. It just happened.

Now, huddling in the rain, an idea flashed into my mind. I pushed the wet hair off my forehead and rose to my feet.

Last summer The Beast had carried us both back in time.

This time, for some reason, Ashley had been pulled back alone.

I imagined her, all by herself, stuck in some other time, her blue eyes filling with tears. She'd be a mess without me.

She might even be in trouble.

I had to help her. But I couldn't do it alone. I needed a helper.

I had to get back to The Beast.

Maybe P.D. was standing there on the platform, waiting for me.

Maybe the old ghost could help me rescue Ashley from the past.

I was so wrapped up in my thoughts that I nearly didn't duck down in time to hide from the guards on their return trip.

I hit the ground seconds before they passed.

Close call.

One of them stepped off the path.

He was marching straight toward the wastebasket.

Straight toward me.

The beam of his flashlight shone into my face.

"Well, lookee here what I found!" he called out to his partner.

6

The guard dived toward me.

I knew I should run while I still had the chance, but my sneakers felt rooted to the spot.

Besides, my right foot had fallen fast asleep. I'd have to drag it after me, like a sack of potatoes.

Maybe my brain was asleep, too, because I didn't even have a good story ready to blurt out to him.

I wasn't even sure I'd be able to talk. My tongue felt as if it had swollen to the size of knockwurst!

The guard bent down. His tall shadow fell across me.

I squeezed my eyes shut, waiting for him to grab me by my shoulders and yank me to my feet.

But nothing happened.

I opened my eyes, one at a time.

The guard had straightened up again.

He was staring down into his hand.

"Well, lookee what I found," he called out to his buddy. "It's a genuine silver dollar."

I practically fainted in relief as he ran over to show his partner.

"What do you know! It's a nineteen twenty-eight!" he exclaimed. "I didn't know there were any of these around anymore."

"You might be a rich man yet!" His partner chuckled as the two of them strolled off.

It was drizzling harder now. My shirt and pants were sopping, and my sneaker soles were coated with mud.

I waited until the guards were out of earshot. Then I rose slowly, stamping my foot to work out the pins and needles.

Then I made a beeline for The Beast.

The park felt eerie. The buildings and rides hunched behind a thin curtain of falling rain.

I kept to the grassy alley behind the buildings. I didn't want to run into any more guards. My sneakers squeaked as I made my way across the wet grass.

Running wasn't easy. My breath came out in painful little puffs. I had that heavy feeling again, as if I had a rock weighing me down.

I had a bad feeling about Ashley. I had the feeling that she needed me.

I had to get to her. I had to help her before something really terrible happened.

I wasn't doing so great myself. I was wet all the way through to my underwear, and I was shivering from the cold.

Then I heard something.

I pulled up short and held my breath, listening.

I heard the splatter of raindrops, sifting down like fine sand on the rooftops of the buildings and on the leaves of the small trees.

But I heard something else, too.

The ghostly clatter of wheels over wooden tracks.

I'd know that sound anywhere.

The rattle of the coaster wheels, the hollow sound of the empty cars rolling over the creaking wooden tracks.

The Beast!

I dashed up the ramp and skidded to a stop on the platform.

Then I saw him. He stood with his hands on the control levers, his head lowered.

He wore the same big, old-fashioned-looking overalls over a black, long-sleeved sweater.

I shivered as a sudden damp gust of wind swept across the platform. It lifted his white hair up around his head like a loose, silvery hood.

My heart was pounding. I cleared my throat nervously.

He didn't glance up from the controls.

I guess he hadn't noticed me yet. I wasn't sure I even wanted him to notice me.

There was still time to turn around and run.

I felt the hairs on the back of my neck standing on end. But I stood my ground.

Sure, I had come back here to find P.D. because somehow I knew that he was my only hope.

But that didn't mean I had the nerve to approach him.

I found myself wishing Ashley were here.

She would have just bopped up to him and said, "Hey, P.D., how's it going?"

I wasn't feeling very bold. I was cold and wet and exhausted, and scared out of my mind.

But I swallowed hard and opened my mouth to speak to the ghost.

7

"H-Hi," I squeaked out feebly.

P.D. raised his eyes from the control panel and stared at me. His eyes were dark and sunk deep in his pale face. His lips remained in a straight, grim line.

Over the sound of the rain pelting the platform roof, I could hear the coaster cars as they clattered somewhere above us.

Still he didn't say anything.

This year my hair was shorter on the sides but longer in the back. And I'd grown three-and-a-quarter inches.

Was it possible he didn't recognize me?

I pushed the damp hair off my forehead and stammered, "Don't you remember me?"

"Of course I remember you, James," his voice boomed back at me. It seemed to stir up the mist that swirled across the platform like wisps of smoke from a cauldron.

"Great!" I broke into a relieved grin and moved a few steps closer to him.

The moisture in the air had beaded on the white hairs of his beard and mustache. It looked like hundreds of tiny diamonds, sparkling in the darkness.

He began to speak, his voice a low rumble in the smoky mist. "I'll never forget that night in Firelight Park. You and your cousin Ashley really showed me a good time." His lips curled into a smile. "I have very warm memories of that night."

He patted his belly. "I must have eaten half a dozen Coney Island Dogs. You were flush that night."

"Flush?" I asked.

"Rich!" He threw back his head and laughed, the sound bouncing off the platform roof.

It wasn't that I was rich. It was just that a little bit of modern money went a long way back then. I mean, a hot dog cost only three cents.

P.D. went on, "You had more money than any kid I had ever met. Then again, most kids I knew were as dirt poor as I was. Still, it was the best night I'd ever spent in Firelight Park."

His face clouded over. "The last one, too," he said sadly.

I nodded without saying anything.

What could I say? *I'm real sorry you died?*

"It's good to see you again, James. But why are you here?" he asked.

And then it all came spilling out of me. How I had opened my eyes after the ride was over and Ashley was gone.

"That's why I came back here," I explained, "to get your help."

He stroked his long white beard in silence. When he spoke at last, his voice was a ghostly whisper. "I still don't understand, James. How is it that you think I can help you?"

"You're my only hope, P.D.," I pleaded. "I think you're the key—"

I broke off as two security guards came up behind me through the mist. "What are you doing here?" one of them demanded.

"I'm talking to P.D.," I explained, gesturing toward the control booth.

The two guards stared into the fog swirling across the platform.

"Talking to *who?*" the guard demanded.

I turned over to the control panel. Only a misty swirl remained where P.D. had stood moments ago.

The ghost had vanished.

But the guards were definitely there.

And they had me.

I was trapped.

8

One on either side of me, the guards firmly guided me down the ramp, away from The Beast.

I threw a helpless look over my shoulder.

"Don't you know the park is closed, son?" one asked.

"This is trespassing," the other added. "You're breaking the law."

"We'll have to call your mom and dad," the other guard said. "They won't be too pleased."

I let them practically carry me through the park, past the silent rides, the darkened booths.

I don't think I could have walked on my own

even if they'd let me. My legs felt limp and lifeless.

I hung my head.

Ashley was really in trouble now.

How could I get Ashley back if they were going to make me leave the park?

And what was I supposed to tell my parents when they came to get me?

What was I supposed to tell Ashley's parents?

I was in serious trouble. And Ashley wouldn't even be there to help me.

Ashley always came up with great explanations to keep us out of trouble. She handles grown-ups like a real pro. Parents love her, especially mine. In fact, they hardly ever get mad at me when she is visiting.

But they'd get mad at me now, that was for sure.

The dim lights glistened in the rain puddles as they marched me down International Street toward the main gate.

They'd be taking me to their cold, brightly lit security office. They'd phone my parents. There would be all sorts of questions.

I felt tears sting my eyes. Maybe I'd never see my cousin again.

The rain fell harder. The fog seemed to thicken near the ground, swirling and bubbling around our feet.

Then it shot up like a geyser in front of us, towering over our heads.

I gasped in surprise as the fog slowly took on the shape of a face. I stared at two huge hollow eyes and a long flaming beard. The face began to swarm with millions of insects, feasting on its flesh.

A smell like rotted flesh filled the air. The eyes widened, boring into me. Then the disgusting insects poured out of the eye sockets, spilling over onto the pavement at our feet.

The gruesome skull opened its mouth wide and let out a bellowing howl.

9

Horrified, the guards let go of me and staggered back.

I didn't think. I just ran.

I ran into the thick, swirling fog. Then I dived into the bushes and hid.

I heard footsteps splattering on the pavement. Other men came running to the rescue. Doors squeaked open and slammed shut. Flashlight arcs crisscrossed the gloomy wetness.

I heard a babble of conversation from the guards.

"I tell you, it was some kind of a weird monster."

"A giant zombie or something! You shoulda seen the size of it!"

Acknowledge,

Talk,

Teach,

Act

"You're crazy!"

"No! We're not makin' this up."

"Yeah, sure. You two guys watch too many horror movies."

"I know what I saw!"

"Then what did you see?"

"I don't know! But I'll be seeing it in my dreams!"

"Hey, where's the kid?"

"The kid? He was here just a minute ago."

"He must have slipped away."

Then more footsteps. More scrambling and shouting. Flashlights cutting through the rain.

I huddled in the bushes, shivering, hoping they wouldn't find me.

I bent down to tie one sopping shoelace—when I felt someone tap me on the shoulder.

My heart stopped beating.

Oh, no!

I spun around to see P.D. He grinned like a small boy. "Pretty good show, eh?" he whispered.

I sagged in relief. "That was you back there? You scared me to death!"

"Thank you." He snickered. "I'm glad to see I still have it in me. I haven't haunted anyone for years. That was fun."

He rose beside me and reached a hand down to pull me up. He was so strong. It was as if I had flown to my feet.

"Come on," he said. "We haven't got much time."

"Does this mean you can help me?" I asked hopefully.

"It means I'm going to try," he replied. "There have been some strange events lately."

"Strange?" I echoed.

He nodded, stroking his long white beard. "Objects from the past that have strayed into the present."

"What kind of objects?" I wanted to know.

"A lady's umbrella. Some loose change. Random odds and ends from the old days . . ." he trailed off. "We must get back to The Beast. The Beast is our only hope."

I followed his ghostly form through the rain. It was hard going. I had to dodge puddles and guards. Both seemed to be everywhere.

It was hard keeping up with P.D.'s long, stalking stride. My soaked sneakers slipped and slid through the mud as I scrambled after him.

Sometimes his body seemed to blend into the rain and mist. A few times I nearly lost him.

44

But at least I knew where we were going. We were going back to The Beast.

Finally I staggered up the ramp and onto the platform.

P.D. was already there, standing at the controls. He brought the train of cars rattling swiftly around to the loading station. "Hurry," he urged me, "before they find you. Get in the coaster."

My glance flickered over the rows of shiny wet seats. Where should I sit?

Reading my mind, P.D. knew the answer. "Take Ashley's seat," he instructed me. "Might as well sit in the exact spot she disappeared from."

I nodded and ran to the head of the coaster. I jumped into Ashley's seat and brought the safety bar down with a crash.

The Beast began to roll.

It felt creepy, sitting here in the rain, all by myself at the head of a train full of empty cars. The coaster clattered up the slick, dark tracks.

A thought flashed through my mind: *The park closes The Beast when it rains this hard.*

Too late to worry about that now.

Besides, I was way beyond worry. Halfway to terrified.

My heart was pounding painfully. I gripped the cold slippery bar so hard my hands hurt. Higher and higher into the rainy darkness I climbed.

I couldn't see anything. Only a swirling darkness.

Suddenly the car whipped forward and picked up speed. Faster and faster, roaring up the tracks.

I found myself bracing for the moment when I would reach the peak of that first hill and plunge down.

Then I thought, *Shouldn't we have reached the peak by now?*

But that moment didn't come. And didn't come. And each moment it didn't come, the terror inside me grew.

Faster and faster and higher and higher, like a missile shooting blindly into the darkness.

The wind whistled past me. My shoulders were stiff and aching. My ears popped painfully.

Then I opened my mouth and screamed as the wheels ripped loose from the track—and the car rocketed into the sky.

10

I shut my eyes. I waited for the crash.

Waited.

The car came to a gentle stop.

I opened my eyes to total darkness.

"Hey—!" My voice came out choked and tiny. "Where am I?"

A door opened. Light poured in.

I blinked rapidly and squinted into the light.

"Huh?" I found myself sitting in some sort of booth or capsule. It was round, like a hollowed-out sphere, with thick metal seams studded with hefty bolts.

The seat felt dry and soft, upholstered in rich red velvet.

Before me lay a control panel, dials and knobs and levers.

A large wheel, like something from a submarine, jutted out of the wall to the right of me, half a foot above my head.

Where in the world am I? What happened to the roller coaster car?

Before I could cry out, a white-gloved hand shot through the open porthole door. It grabbed me by my collar.

"Hey—whoa!" I blurted as I was yanked out of the capsule and out into the open.

A man towered over me, examining me with cold, dark eyes. Something in his expression made me feel like a bug squirming beneath a glass.

I tried to be brave and stare back at him. But it was hard because I was so completely terrified.

His black hair was slicked back. On his upper lip was a mustache so thin it looked as if he had drawn it on with a pen. He wore gray flannel trousers and a red pin-striped vest over a starched white shirt.

He looked neat and respectable enough. But

there was something slightly strange about him.

Something I couldn't quite put my finger on.

"You're a good one!" he cried.

A good *what?* I opened my mouth to ask him just that.

"Be quiet!" he bellowed before I got a word out.

I snapped my mouth shut and stared at him. His dark eyes burned into mine.

"Take off those clothes!" he shouted.

"Excuse me?" I cried.

My clothes were sopping wet from the rain, but there was no way I was going to take them off. I didn't even change in the locker room in front of kids I had known all my life.

The man grabbed me and started to pull my shirt off over my head.

"All right, all right!" I protested, wriggling away from him. I wasn't going to let *him* undress me, that was for sure.

I jumped behind the capsule where he couldn't see me and pulled off my clothes. Then I threw them over to the man.

Panic surged through me as I watched him scoop up my clothes and take them over to a closet. I shivered as he unlocked the closet with a key from a heavy, jangling key ring.

While he worked, he muttered to himself. I couldn't make out any words.

He stuffed my clothes into the closet. Then he returned with a pile of shiny, silvery fabric. He thrust it at me.

"Put it on!" he snapped.

"But—"

"Just do it," he ordered. "Let's not start off on the wrong foot. There's no room for rebels and upstarts in my show."

What show?

With cold, trembling hands I climbed into the silver outfit.

It was all one piece, made of a silver fabric. A row of silver hooks ran from the collar to the inside ankle of the right leg. My hands were trembling so hard, I kept mismatching the hooks and eyes.

Finally I managed to do up every last hook and eye. I looked down at myself.

I was so embarrassed!

I like my clothes loose, preferably baggy. This outfit was nearly as tight as a wetsuit.

I wouldn't wear something like this—even on Halloween.

The man walked around me, studying me. He seemed to be pleased.

"Good," he muttered with a sharp nod. "Very good. No traces. No traces whatsoever."

No traces?

"No traces of what?" I asked in a squeaky voice.

"SHUT UP!" he shouted and slapped me across the face.

I rubbed my stinging cheek as tears sprang to my eyes.

He smiled almost kindly then and waggled his finger at me. "Be a good boy and that won't happen again," he told me in a soft, silky voice.

I nodded numbly.

Then he grabbed my arm and led me away from the capsule.

I stared back at it. That capsule, whatever it was, was my only link to my real life. My only way out of this nightmare.

We were in a huge building, as big as an airplane hangar. It was cold and poorly lit. But I could make out low walls on either side of us as he dragged me down a long hall.

Doors flashed past me, most of them closed. The open rooms were too dark to see inside.

I didn't have time to look, anyway. Every time I slowed down to get a look, the man gave my arm such a jerk it practically came out of its socket.

I heard muffled voices coming from behind the low walls.

Someone shouted. A girl.

Not Ashley.

Several men and women stood talking in the hall. The men wore striped shirts and baggy pants, pleated in front. The women wore long dark dresses down to their ankles, with big shoulder pads. They wore dark lipstick.

The fashions told me what I had already guessed. I had traveled back in time. But to when?

Where was I? What was going on? I had absolutely no idea.

The people fell silent as we edged past them. I could feel their eyes on me, following me.

I wanted to cry out for help. But their expressions were cold and unfriendly.

They were staring at me as if I were from Mars.

The hall widened as we passed a giant glass tank filled with water. Long tendrils of pink and orange seaweed floated in the water.

A large fish fluttered out from behind a huge purple sea fan.

I looked at the fish more closely. My heart nearly stopped.

The fish had a human face! The face of a boy, eight or nine years old.

The body was covered with shimmering green scales. And he had a long swishing fish-tail in place of legs and feet.

"You like my little pet?" the man asked me.

I stared after it in horror as the man dragged me away.

I heard my voice rise to a panicky shriek. "What *is* this place?"

His only answer was an arm-wrenching yank.

I cast one last backward glance at the tank. The fish-boy had swum up to the glass and pressed his face to it. He stared at me, with large, dark, terrified eyes.

A stream of bubbles flew out of his mouth.

He was mouthing a word through the water and the glass, trying desperately to be understood.

"Run!" he said. "Run!"

11

The man tightened his grip on me. There was no way I could run.

Where was I going? What was going to happen to me?

Would I wind up in a fish tank like that boy?

Finally the man pushed me through a dark doorway. I stumbled and fell up a set of stairs. "Climb up," he ordered. I crawled up the stairs on my hands and knees.

I stood up slowly, my heart thundering in my chest.

It was dark and stuffy. I reached out. My trembling fingers felt a drape or a curtain.

I groped around, searching frantically for an

opening in the curtain. Then, with a sickening jolt, I became aware of others beside me in the darkness, breathing softly.

I shrank back into my own space and froze, waiting, listening.

I heard a sniffling sound. Then a cry.

A human cry.

I sagged in relief. Whoever it was sounded as scared as I was.

"Hurry, hurry! Ladies and gents!" A loud voice pierced the darkness.

"Step right up and see the A-mazing Chee-ildren of the Future! You won't believe your eyes. They will astound and astonish you. Ask them questions. Ask them anything you like. You won't believe your ears as they tell you of the untold wonders of the near and distant future."

Suddenly bright lights hit my eyes as the curtain scraped back.

A crowd of people in old-fashioned clothes gasped and jostled each other to get a better look.

They were gawking and shouting, pointing up through a row of thick metal bars.

I was standing in a large cage!

In the cage with me stood a dozen or so other kids.

Some were dressed in silvery costumes like mine. Others wore jumpsuits and helmets that resembled space suits in bad science fiction movies. The kid to my left was crying and wiping his nose on his silver sleeve.

But no one noticed or cared.

"Ladies and gents, feast your eyes on Captain Time's Children of the Future." The man who had brought me here now stood to one side of the cage talking to the audience.

He wore a blue blazer and a white captain's hat with a shiny black visor. He thumped the cage bars with a wooden club.

"Go ahead, ladies and gents, don't be afraid. Ask them anything you like. They won't bite."

The crowd murmured softly and continued to stare up at us in disbelief.

"How do you sleep in the future?" a young woman piped up. "In regular beds—or what?"

"Standing up," the kid on the other side of me answered in a droning voice, like a robot. "With our eyes open. Children of the Future never dream. Never have nightmares. It is a perfect world. We are lucky Children of the Future."

"What do you eat?" a man called out from the back of the room.

"We do not eat food," a skinny kid answered in that same zombie-like voice. "The Children of the Future eat only vitamin pills! We are very healthy. We are lucky Children of the Future."

No sleep. No food. What kind of a future did these kids come from? Not *my* future.

What was wrong with them?

"Vitamin pills?" an audience member piped up. "I don't believe it."

"You're totally right not to believe it!" a girl's voice rang out from behind me.

The noise level of the crowd rose.

"Don't listen to him!" the girl went on. "Kids of the future eat and dream and sleep just like you do. We eat food, too. We eat junk food. Lots of junk food. Fast food, we call it. Microwave burritos and frozen garbage pizza."

My heart leaped. There was only one person I knew who liked frozen garbage pizza.

"Ashley!" I shouted over the rising noise of the crowd. "Ashley—I'm here!"

12

"James!"

Ashley pushed her way through the cage. Grabbing my hand, she squeezed it hard as if she were making sure I was real.

I squeezed back. It was great to see her.

My cousin was wearing a silver outfit like mine. Her long blond hair was tucked up into an ugly silver bonnet. It fit tight like a bathing cap.

"Can you believe it, James?" she whispered. "We're the kids of the future!"

A woman tapped the bars with the tip of her umbrella. "What's that girl have on her teeth?" she asked.

"It's a mark of royalty of a princess from the future," Captain Time explained.

"No, it's not," Ashley broke in. "They're braces."

"False teeth?" someone asked.

"No," Ashley corrected him. "Braces to straighten my teeth. You know, from an orthodontist? Kids of the future have straight teeth, whether they want them or not."

The people in the crowd murmured.

"Don't listen to her!" Captain Time spoke out. "This girl is a princess from the future. That strange pink and purple substance on her teeth was put on her teeth at birth. It's the special mark of a princess!"

"What is that man talking about?" I whispered.

Ashley frowned. "Actually, that's what I told him when he first yanked me out of the capsule. I think he likes the idea that he's caught himself a real live princess for his freak show."

"Let's hear a round of applause for the Princess of the Future!" Captain Time shouted.

Scattered clapping.

I don't think they believed him.

I don't think they believed any of us was

from the future. Even though Ashley and I really were.

"Do kids have to go to school in the future?" a boy in the audience wanted to know.

"No!" another member of the zombie troupe answered. "In the future children don't have to go to school. They can sit at home and watch radio with pictures! Children of the Future are lucky."

"Yay for the future!" The kids in the audience broke out in cheers.

"I only wish," I whispered to Ashley.

She shrugged. "Yeah, well, the Captain has his own ideas about the future."

Another question quickly followed the last. "How do you get around? By electric car?"

"No!" a silver-costumed girl responded. "Children of the Future travel by jet pack! We can fly anywhere we like, any time we like."

"Gimme a break!" I murmured.

"Is there a cure for the flu?" a man in the crowd asked.

"In the future," one of the other kids spoke up, "there is no disease. Everyone takes an anti-disease pill, and no one ever gets sick."

"Yeah, right," Ashley muttered under her breath.

The crowd didn't seem to believe this any more than we did.

They began to grumble. A few started to hiss and boo at us.

I felt something jab me in the leg. A man was poking his cane through the bars at me. I tried to kick him.

"Animal!" the man shouted, shaking his fist at me. "Freak."

The others joined in, calling us names. I felt something sting my forehead.

I reached up and rubbed the spot.

I looked down at the floor near my feet. It was a peanut. Someone had actually thrown a peanut at me!

Kids in the audience began throwing them by the handful.

Ashley and I ducked.

"All right, ladies and gents!" Captain Time shouted, ringing the curtain shut. "Show's over. Next show starts in twenty minutes. Get in line and purchase your tickets. Two bits a piece."

Ashley grabbed my hand.

"We have to do this again in twenty minutes?" I asked.

"Can you believe it? We have to do eighteen shows a day, James," she told me. I followed her off the platform and into a room backstage.

All the kids crowded into it, grumbling and whining. There wasn't any furniture. Just bales of hay. Loose hay was spread on the packed dirt floor.

The kids threw themselves down on the bales of hay.

Most of them were scrawny. Their faces were pale and their eyes were hollow. Kids of the future didn't look too lucky to me. Or too healthy, either.

I pulled Ashley into the corner. I had a ton of questions on my mind.

But she put a finger to my mouth. "Not here," she warned. "The Captain's spies are everywhere.

She grabbed my hand and led me into another room no bigger than a large closet. It held a single beat-up couch.

"The Captain lets me use this room," she explained, taking a seat on the musty-smelling couch. "Because I'm the Princess."

"At least he gives you the princess treatment. Me, he handled like a punching bag."

Ashley shook her head. "You've just got to do what he says, James. Do what he says and he won't hurt you. Sit down." She patted the cushion next to her, and a puff of dust rose up.

I sank down next to her. "So what is this place?" I demanded.

"A carnival in Firelight Park," she explained in a tired voice. "We're definitely back in the park again. I don't know what year. It's nineteen thirty-something."

I nodded quickly. "Do all these kids come from the future?"

"I can't tell. Most of them are so tired and confused, I'm not sure they even know anymore. A lot of them are just runaways and orphans from this time. Captain Time tries to make all of us give the same stupid answers, anyway."

"Who is this guy?" I asked.

"He runs the carnival," Ashley explained. "He's the son of the owner of Firelight Park. His father lets him run this carnival. He uses the money the carnival earns for his experiments."

"Experiments?" I asked. I remembered with a shudder the fish-boy in the tank.

"All kinds of experiments," Ashley explained. "But mostly, time travel."

I nodded. "I *knew* that capsule was a time machine the moment I saw it."

Ashley sighed. "What are we going to do, James?"

It seemed pretty simple to me. "Ask Captain Time to send us back to the future?" I suggested.

She tossed her head impatiently. "Don't you think I've already asked him a dozen times? He won't do it, James. I've begged. The harder I beg, the louder he says no. He wants to keep us here. Like prisoners."

I thought of the bales of hay in the room next door. "Like wild animals in a zoo. Then we've got to find a way to escape. We—"

"There you are, Princess!" Captain Time strode briskly into the room.

"Ah, Princess. Entertaining our newest time traveler, I see." He flashed an oily smile and ran one white-gloved finger over the pencil-thin mustache.

"This is my cousin, James Dickson. Say hello

64

to the nice man, James." Ashley shot me a meaningful look.

His dark eyes lit up. "Cousins! That's a first. I've transported cousins! Brilliant! Wait till I tell Father. He won't believe me. None of them believe me. They think it's all a hoax.

"I am good, aren't I?" he demanded. "I can transport human life through time. I'm a genius. A genius!"

"Since you are a genius," I suggested politely, "why don't you return us back to our own time?"

"Why would I want to do that?" he asked.

"Because," I explained to him carefully, "we want to go back to our own time and place." Then I got braver. "You're a kidnapper if you keep us here against our wills."

"Send us back," Ashley joined in boldly. "Send us back, and we won't press charges."

He smiled sadly. "Believe me, Princess. I'd *love* to send you back."

"Great!" we both exclaimed.

"There's only one little problem," he added, shaking his head. "I don't know how."

13

I sprang to my feet. "You mean to say you can bring people back in time, but you can't *return* them?" I cried.

"Yes," he replied sadly. "I've got the *back* part down pat. It's the *forward* part I'm a little shaky on. Can't get the hang of it at all."

He pulled a gold watch from the pocket of his trousers. He tapped the glass face. "It's time to rest up. Only ten more minutes until the next show."

"What if we don't want to do the show?" I demanded.

He paused in the doorway and turned. "But you must. You have no choice. And you, Princess"—he waved long white-gloved fingers over at Ashley—"kindly stop making up your own answers to the audience's questions. Just stick to the script."

Ashley snatched off her silver cap and shook out her blond hair. "And what if we don't stick to the script?" she demanded.

"Listen to me." His voice fell to a deadly whisper as he moved closer to her. "Princess or no princess, you will do as I tell you. Is that crystal clear, Princess?"

"Yes, sir!" Ashley gave a sullen salute.

Captain Time glared at Ashley. "The last troublemaker found himself in a large tank of cold water covered with slimy green scales."

So I was right! Captain Time *did* turn that boy into a fish!

Captain Time might be a genius. But he was an evil genius, I decided.

"Do we have an understanding?" he asked.

We both turned to the Captain at the same time and snapped to attention.

"Yes, sir!" we barked.

"As soon as Captain Time left, I ran to the door and peered around the corner.

The hallway was empty.

I signaled to Ashley. "Come on. Let's go!"

Her eyes widened in fear. "You heard him. The show's about to begin. We have to get ready. He always starts on time."

"Who cares? You mean to tell me you want to sit around here for the rest of your life doing eighteen shows a day? Let's get out of here," I urged.

Ashley tucked her hair neatly back into her cap and sighed wearily. "Forget it, James."

I shook my head in confusion. "Forget it?" I repeated. "You mean you don't want to escape?"

"It's not that I don't want to, James. But how far do you think we would get wearing these trick-or-treat costumes?"

I stared at our costumes. We sparkled like a pair of foil-wrapped human hoagies.

Ashley had a point.

"Besides," she added sensibly, "getting out of here won't help us get back to our time."

I nodded and chewed my lower lip. "The time machine is in this building—right?"

"So the best thing we can do until we can get near it," Ashley explained, "is to behave like Captain Time's good little Children of the

Future. That way he'll trust us. Or at least forget about us—"

"Long enough for us to find a way out of here back to our own time," I finished for her.

So Ashley and I huddled together on the couch while she gave me a crash course on how to answer the audience's questions about the future.

What we ate. What we wore. How we slept. How we traveled. She even demonstrated how we danced.

The dance was especially dumb.

But I concentrated hard. I learned every step and memorized every word of Captain Time's script for good, little, lucky Children of the Future.

It was just like studying for a unit test.

Only this was one test we had to pass. If we didn't, we both knew what would happen.

We would be left back.

Back in the past.

Forever.

14

I lay awake for hours. Bits of straw scratched my bare skin through the thin silver fabric of my costume.

I breathed deeply, fake snoozing, until I thought the whole roomful of kids was sound asleep.

Then I rolled over and shook Ashley awake.

My cousin usually doesn't react well when you wake her up in the middle of the night.

When our families spent Christmas together one time years ago, we made a pact to wake up at three o'clock in the morning. We wanted to see if we could catch Santa Claus in the act.

I went into Ashley's room to wake her up—and she let out a scream that shook the house!

No silent night for us.

Both families came tearing in to see what terrible thing had happened.

There I was, standing in my pajamas in the middle of the room. I mumbled something about Ashley having a nightmare. Pretty lame.

Now, lying on the straw-strewn floor of our prison, I shook Ashley's shoulder. She wouldn't budge. Maybe she was dreaming about being home again.

This was no time to dream. We were in the middle of a nightmare.

Finally I took a piece of straw and stuck it up her nose.

Good move.

She wiggled her nose and sat up, glaring at me. "James—"

"Shhhhhh." I pressed my hand over her mouth. She stared at me with wide, frightened eyes.

Around us, the other Children of the Future continued to snore.

Slowly I took my hand off her mouth and helped her to her feet.

We made our way through the dark room.

Earlier, after the last show of the night, two tough-looking men in black bowler hats led us down the long hallway to another room. We sat at long picnic tables while they served us what looked like pig swill.

Not that I've ever actually seen pig swill. But that's what I imagined it looked like. It was bits of fat and gristle swimming in gray, greasy goop.

It made the food in my school cafeteria look like a gourmet feast.

I couldn't believe that the other kids were shoveling the swill into their mouths with both hands.

No way would Ashley and I touch the food. When no one was looking, we both dumped it onto the floor beneath the table.

Afterward, the same two men herded us back into the room behind the stage. They told us to shut up and go to sleep.

Most of the kids had fallen into an exhausted sleep immediately.

So far so good.

The door to the room behind the stage wasn't

locked. Captain Time probably figured there was nowhere we could go.

I heard a sudden loud snort—and froze.

A guard was asleep on duty. His chair tipped back against the wall. His bowler hat covered his eyes. His mouth was wide open, sucking in great big mouthfuls of air as he snored.

I tiptoed past him, down the long hall, past the room where we had eaten, past the giant fish tank.

We stopped long enough to peer inside. It was empty except for the tall orange and yellow fronds of seaweed waving eerily to and fro.

What had happened to the fish-boy?

Maybe the Captain let him out of the tank at night to sleep in a real bed.

We passed the rows of doors and finally came out into a larger room. Ashley pointed.

In the far corner stood the time machine.

A greenish-yellow light shone out of its porthole windows. We ran toward it. As we approached, we heard a high-pitched hum.

The Captain had made it easier for us. He had left the power on.

Ashley ran ahead of me and yanked open the

round door. "Come on, James," she urged in a hushed whisper. "Let's go."

I hesitated. "Go where? How?"

But Ashley didn't seem to care. She was already dropping onto the red seat. She patted the cushion next to her. "Out of here. That's all that matters."

I wasn't so sure.

"Hurry, James!"

I stared hard at her. Her eyes were huge and glassy. Was this just another adventure to her? Didn't she realize how serious this was?

Reluctantly I climbed in beside her. I kept the door open. I hate closed-in spaces. I don't even like sleeping in a tent.

"Okay, James," she said in a businesslike way. "Let's try fiddling with some of these knobs."

I stared helplessly at the panel. Not a single one of the knobs, dials, or levers was labeled.

Who knew what they did? Only the Captain. And the Captain was fast asleep.

I hoped.

Ashley leaned over me and swung the door shut.

"Wouldn't want to fall out in the middle of time," she muttered.

Very funny.

Then she reached for the nearest knob. "Let's try twisting this cute little knob to the left," she chatted nervously. "Maybe the machine is programmed. Maybe the machine will just reverse itself and send us back."

"Ashley!" I warned.

"What harm could it do?" she asked innocently.

15

I pulled her hand off the knob. "Have you lost your mind completely?" I demanded.

Her blue eyes narrowed to slits. "No, James, but I think you have. Don't you want to get out of here?"

"Of course I do. But I want to get out of here in one piece. You don't know the first thing about time travel, Ashley. I do. I've been reading all about it ever since last summer. Time travel can be very dangerous," I told her.

She sat back in her seat and folded her arms across her silver jumpsuit. She rolled her eyes.

"All right. Tell me how dangerous."

I figured I'd tell it to her straight.

"Time travel involves taking huge risks," I told her. "But we don't even have a way to judge the risk. We're traveling blind. We have no idea where we might wind up."

"So?"

"So? So we could easily pop up in the middle of a rock! Or at the bottom of an ocean. Or who knows where!" I explained.

"All right, James." She sighed. "I think I get the idea. But maybe we'd pop up safe and sound back at Paramount's Kings Island. Or in our own beds. Or in your mom's kitchen, just as she's taking one of her chocolate pies out of the oven."

I nodded reluctantly. I could almost smell the chocolate pie.

Ashley's blue eyes sparkled. "Then don't you think it's worth the risk, James? I do. I say we go for it!"

She reached for the knob.

I eyed her tensely. But this time I didn't try and stop her.

I knew she wasn't going to give up until she had tried to use the machine.

I held my breath as she twisted the knob.

The arrows on the dials didn't move.

Nothing happened.

We stared at each other in disappointment.

"Okay, try that blue lever next to it," I suggested.

Might as well keep at it until we got results.

She pushed it down, an inch. We both braced ourselves.

Again, nothing happened.

She moved it another inch.

The arrows on the dials started twitching. A high-pitched hum rose around us.

Ashley turned to stare at me. Her blue eyes widened. Her face twisted in horror.

"Noooooo!" she wailed.

Spidery lines sprouted at the corners of her eyes and crawled down her cheeks, past her ears and onto her neck. As her skin wrinkled, her cheeks and ears sagged.

Liver spots spread across her forehead and scalp. Her hair turned gray and fell out in clumps.

Ashley cried out for help. Three of her teeth blackened and fell out over her gums. She caught them in a hand that looked like a claw.

My cries joined hers. I felt the flesh shrink on my bones, and my spine curve like a bow.

I felt my right eye droop down onto my cheek. Everything got blurry then.

I heard an old man moaning. The old man was me.

Part of me knew we were both aging at a rapid speed. That same part knew that if we didn't do something soon to reverse it—we would die and turn into skeletons in seconds.

But most of me just wanted to shrivel up and die—and get it over with!

Every bone in my body ached. I couldn't see. I was too weak to scream.

With what remained of my strength, I fell on the blue lever and struggled to pull it back up.

"Pull it, James! Pull it!" Ashley croaked.

"I can't!" I croaked back. "I can't!"

16

The lever was stuck.

I couldn't budge it.

I opened my mouth and flapped my gums at Ashley, "Help me pull!"

Her knobby old head trembled, and she smacked her lips.

"Help me pull it!" I pleaded.

Ashley lowered her wrinkled, spotted hands over mine.

"Pull! Pull!" I gasped.

Finally the lever began to edge back up. A fraction of an inch at a time.

The needles in the dials stopped twitching.

The deafening roar of the machine died down to a faint hum.

I glanced over at my cousin. With a surge of relief I saw that she was getting younger.

Her wrinkled skin grew smooth and rosy pink, and her teeth popped back into her head.

Her hair returned to silken, shiny blond.

Her hands grew plump and strong-looking.

While all this was happening, I could feel my own spine growing stronger and straighter. My skin tightened on my bones. It was great to feel the teeth in my head once again.

Our hands fell away from the lever.

"Whew!"

"You're not kidding!"

I flopped back against the velvet cushions, exhausted.

"Wow. That was close." Ashley panted. "Oh, James, I don't think I ever want to get old."

"Me, neither," I agreed. Then I grinned at her. "You should have seen how gross you looked!" I teased.

"Me?" She gave an outraged squeal.

"You looked like a shriveled-up old raisin!"

"If I was a raisin, James, you were a prune!"

"Fine," I said. "We both looked pretty gross. Touch that blue lever again and I'll break all ten of your fingers."

"Okay," she agreed. "I'll just try turning this big wheel here, instead."

Before I could stop her, Ashley had reached up and spun the heavy wheel above our heads.

The machine began to rumble.

We stared at each other. Something was definitely happening.

The machine began to vibrate. The light dimmed from yellow-green to deep blood red.

"Whoa!" I braced myself.

"What's happening, James?" Ashley cried out.

The red light began to blink and the vibrations shook us. The machine was shuddering and rumbling.

"Maybe it's working!" I called out over the roar of the machine.

"1990s, here we come!" Ashley exclaimed, pumping her fist in the air in triumph!

After a few seconds the machine fell silent and still. The lights brightened to green.

Where had the machine taken us? I wondered.

My heart beat wildly. Maybe it had worked. Maybe we were back in our time.

I reached over and unlatched the door.

But someone else swung the door open before I got a chance.

Captain Time.

He stood outside the capsule, wearing a long black satin robe and velvet slippers. His black hair was messy from sleep. But he looked wide awake now.

And angry.

He slapped the heavy wooden club into the palm of his hand.

Slap. Slap. Slap.

"Come out of there, you two," he said through gritted teeth.

Ashley and I exchanged looks of pure dread. She gave my hand a quick squeeze.

We both knew we were in major trouble.

We stood before the Captain with our heads lowered. Too bad *fear* doesn't send you hurtling through time. My fear could have carried me clear into the next century!

"Which one of you turned that wheel?" Captain Time demanded.

After a brief nervous silence Ashley piped up, "I did, Captain. Sir," she added meekly.

He chuckled softly. "Thank you, Princess. That wheel sets off the alarm. And the alarm woke me. And here I am. And here you are. What have you to say for yourselves?"

"Sorry?" I tried timidly.

"Not good enough!" he bellowed.

I jumped half a foot.

"I am not happy," Captain Time said. "Not happy at all."

What did that mean?

Once again I pictured the boy in the fish tank. I saw myself swimming beside him.

"We're really, really, sorry!" I insisted.

"Are you really?" He frowned at me. "Well, I'll forgive you this time."

I practically crumpled to the floor. I was so relieved!

No fish tank. Ashley and I were lucky.

This time.

"Now," he announced as he pulled his gold watch out of the pocket of his robe, "it's time to hit the hay. And I do mean hay."

Ashley and I turned away reluctantly from the time machine.

"Listen to me," he told us as he led us back to our little room behind the stage. "I'm not a bad man. I don't want you to be unhappy. Believe me, I wish I could send you both home. I really do."

I wasn't sure I believed him.

But it wasn't like I had any choice.

We trudged down the long hallway. Gas lamps burned eerily in brackets high on the walls, lighting our way back to our prison.

With every step my heart sank deeper in my chest.

"If you keep performing the show and earning me lots of money," he went on, "I can continue my work. Who knows? Maybe some day I'll figure out how to send you back to your own time."

We paused at the door of our room.

"Some day?" Ashley repeated.

The Captain gave a careless heave of his shoulders. "It might take a few years. Now, in you go," he ordered, and slammed the door behind us.

"Some day," Ashley muttered as she tried to make herself a comfortable nest in the straw. "By then our parents will have given up looking for us. Oh, wow. This is terrible. This is worse than being dead."

I shivered miserably. In the early morning hours the room had grown chilly.

As I pulled some straw over my cold and aching bones, I had to agree with her. What a mess. . . .

Just as I was drifting off into a troubled sleep, I felt someone jab me sharply on the shoulder.

I opened my eyes and sat up with a start. I looked around me. No one there. No one but other kids sleeping in the straw.

But someone had been here a moment ago. I knew it. Because someone had left something behind.

It was lying on the straw pillow I had been sleeping on.

A fish.

A dead fish.

I looked at it in horror.

I knew it was a message. A message from Captain Time.

A warning telling me I was going to end up like that fish.

Dead.

18

The next morning Ashley and I escaped.

"Hurry up, James!"

I grabbed the ledge of the high window and hoisted myself up. Then I reached down and dragged my cousin after me.

She slithered over the sill in her silvery suit.

We landed with a thud in an alley outside the carnival building.

I took a deep breath of fresh air and blinked in the sunshine. It was midmorning and we were between performances. Ashley had spied the window on our way to breakfast that morning.

We sneaked away after the last show. Now

we had fifteen minutes until the next show. We had to get away before they noticed we were missing.

Ashley took off down the alley.

I ran after her and blocked her path. "Wait a minute. You said you had a plan?"

She batted her long eyelashes at me. "Of course I have a plan, James. Don't I always have a plan? The plan is to find The Beast."

"That's your plan?" I asked.

"Not much of a plan, is it?" she admitted.

"Well, we found it last year," she added.

I nodded. She was right. Last summer, after searching all over Firelight Park, we had finally come upon The Beast.

The Beast had saved us, whisking us away just in time.

Maybe The Beast could save us again.

"I don't suppose you know where we might find it?" I asked her.

She answered by pointing to the giant Ferris wheel towering over the rest of the park.

"The Ferris wheel?" I repeated. "How will the Ferris wheel help us get back to the present?"

She rolled her eyes. "James, we'll ride the Ferris wheel."

"And the Ferris wheel will—what?" I demanded.

She rolled her eyes. "The Ferris wheel will give us a view of the entire park. Maybe when we're up high, we'll see The Beast. That is, unless you have a better plan, James?"

I shook my head gloomily. My stomach growled. I almost wished I'd eaten this morning's breakfast swill. Almost.

"It's hard to think on an empty stomach," I complained.

I thought of my mother's pot roast. Her spinach lasagna. Chocolate pie.

"Let's go," I said. I grabbed Ashley and ran down the alleyway toward the boardwalk.

We had never been in Firelight Park during the day. The torches standing on top of the poles were out. The sun shone down out of a pale blue, cloudless sky.

It was a great day to visit an amusement park. The boardwalk was packed with people strolling along to the music of an old-fashioned organ.

At first we strolled, too, trying to blend in. It wasn't easy.

The women wore flowered dresses down to

their ankles. The men wore suit jackets. I'd forgotten that in the old days people dressed up
to go to an amusement park.

Was there any such thing as casual clothes?

A group of kids passed us. They wore long,
baggy shorts that fell to below their knees, and
baggy shirts. Instead of sneakers they wore
heavy brown wooden shoes.

"Look!" one of them shouted out, pointing at
us. "Freaks from the future!"

The others laughed. Ashley and I picked up
our pace. Maybe if we slipped through the
crowd like a couple of silver streaks, no one
would notice us.

We ran, losing the kids in the crowd. We
passed a building with a sign that said CRIT-
TER CORRAL.

It looked like a bunch of farm animals—pigs
and cows and geese.

We slowed to a fast walk as we passed a
purple and gold tent. Oriental flute music
floated out of it. A tall man in a turban stood
outside the entrance to the tent. A spotted
snake wrapped him from head to toe.

"Step inside and see the asp that stung
Cleopatra."

"Gross," Ashley said, tugging on my arm. "Come on, James."

I'd never seen an asp before. And I wasn't going to see one now. I didn't have the two cents admission.

We passed a row of carnival booths. Their red and white lights blinked even in the daylight. The brightly colored pennants flying from their rooftops snapped smartly in the breeze.

There were beanbag tosses, pyramids of heavy wooden bottles to topple with big, soft balls. There were sitting ducks waiting to be picked off in shooting galleries. There were prizes, too. Rows of stuffed animals and Kewpie dolls.

It was amazing how little amusement parks had changed over the years.

We passed a man throwing daggers at a woman spinning on a big wooden board.

"Whoa!" I exclaimed as a knife just missed her face.

We passed a dwarf in a purple tank shirt and striped trousers. He was lying on a bed of sharp nails. His muscular arms were folded across his chest. He looked perfectly comfortable lying there on about a thousand razor-sharp nails.

He reached out as we ran by and grabbed Ashley's ankle.

"Hey, girlie," he called out. "For a penny I'll let you step on me."

Ashley stared down at him in disgust.

"I don't have a penny," she told him.

The dwarf grinned. "I'll let you do it for free. Go ahead. It won't hurt me. Step on my chest."

"No, thanks," Ashley stammered, backing off.

We ran on, the dwarf's mocking laughter ringing in our ears.

Then we passed a food stand and I just couldn't help myself. I stopped and stared up at the sign, my poor stomach gurgling like crazy.

CONEY ISLAND DOGS, the sign said. FIT FOR A MILLIONAIRE.

I peered behind the counter.

A row of hot dogs sizzled on the grill. I remembered how delicious they had tasted. And they only cost three cents!

I thought of the mason jar in the bottom drawer of my bureau, filled to the top with pennies I'd never even bothered to take to the bank to trade for bigger money.

I thought of all the times I had dropped a penny and not bothered picking it up. That's how little pennies meant to me.

What I wouldn't give now for three lousy cents.

A woman pushing a toddler in a big wicker stroller stopped beside me to order three Coney Island Dogs.

She hesitated when she saw me staring at her.

"Make that four," she called out to the grill man.

"You poor kid!" she said with a sad shake of her head. "That dreadful Captain Time doesn't take very good care of you kids. It's a wonder the authorities aren't all over him. Here, take it."

She thrust one of her hot dogs into my hand.

I started sputtering thanks, but she waved me away.

"Don't thank me. Just run along before my husband catches us. He hates when I give to beggars."

I gave out with a sickly smile.

First I'm a freak and now I'm a beggar.

I was coming up in the world.

I caught up with Ashley and showed her my prize. I tore it in two and gave her half.

"James! You genius!" she declared as she blew on her half of the steaming hot dog.

We gobbled the dog in seconds. By the time we were finished, we were standing at the foot of the Ferris wheel.

We craned our necks, staring up at the many colored seats, swinging in the breeze. The wheel spun around like a giant wire pinwheel. It looked like fun.

We jumped in line for the next ride, ignoring the stares of the people ahead of us.

They obviously thought we had no business being there. We belonged in the carnival. We weren't supposed to be having fun.

We're *not* having fun! I wanted to tell them.

Our heads turned automatically. We were keeping a lookout for the blue-uniformed guards. Or worse, the Captain's men in their black bowler hats.

By this time Captain Time would have discovered we were gone. Maybe he had already sent out a patrol.

We were both relieved when the wheel started loading for the next ride.

Ashley nudged me. "James," she whispered. "What will we do for tickets?"

"Admission fee covers all rides," I reminded her. She looked relieved.

We climbed into a red seat and fastened the buckles on the brown straps. Then up we swung. The car rocked to and fro, and we moved farther up into the air.

Higher and higher we rose up over the park. The breeze felt wonderful.

I threw back my head and let the warm sun beat down on my face. I had been indoors so long, I was beginning to feel like a fungus! A fungus in a tacky silver suit.

Ashley was enjoying herself, too. She shook her hair loose from the silvery cap and let it whip around in the wind.

The Ferris wheel swung us up to the very top, and there we hung, suspended high above the park.

"Oh, wow!" Ashley breathed. "Isn't it awesome!"

It *was* awesome.

Beneath our dangling feet, the park stretched out in all directions.

"Look!" I shouted to Ashley, pointing. "There's the Shoot-the-Chute."

"Cool!" she exclaimed.

There was the Tilt-a-Whirl, too. Even from way up there, I could hear the screams of its riders, rising and falling like a distant siren. Nearby, the pink and blue merry-go-round spun in the sunshine like a toy top.

For the first time since we arrived, I felt a little hope. There had to be a way out of here, and we could find it.

Then my eye fell on the big warehouse that housed the carnival. An artist had painted a giant portrait of Captain Time in his blue blazer and white hat on the roof. He was grinning and holding up a huge pocket watch.

CAPTAIN TIME'S CHILDREN OF THE FUTURE was written out in fancy script across the bottom.

Captain Time's eyes were huge and black and seemed to be staring straight up at us.

I shuddered.

Ashley poked me hard in the ribs. "There it is, James!" she cried. "I see it! There's The Beast! Now we can go home!"

19

"Where?" I cried excitedly.

She pointed.

Beyond the park's high wooden fence lay a thick grove of trees.

It looked so familiar.

I stared harder at it.

No doubt about it. On the other side of the fence there seemed to be some sort of wooden scaffolding jutting out of the trees.

I remembered the last time we had slipped through a wooden fence to get to The Beast.

And The Beast did run through a thick grove of trees.

My heart began to beat faster.

"Yes!" I cried happily. "There it is!"

The car began to swing back toward the earth.

"Quick, James!" Ashley cried excitedly. "Let's memorize the way there from here."

Each time we swung around, I did my best to figure out a path. Bumper cars, a pond, a green-and-white striped tent with wild animals pictured on it.

Finally we fell dizzily back to the earth for the last time. I was almost sorry to step off the Ferris wheel.

As soon as our feet hit the ground, we were off and running through the crowds.

Past the bumper cars.

Past the pond where little kids dressed in fancy sailor outfits raced model sailboats.

Down the narrow alley between the animal tent and a row of empty cages.

We raced along the high wooden fence, searching for a way through to the other side.

"Here!" I shouted to Ashley.

Someone had dug a deep hole underneath the fence. I fell to my knees and worked my way underneath.

I pulled myself out on the other side. Then

I turned to help Ashley. But she didn't need any help.

My skinny cousin slid underneath like a silver eel.

We dusted off our suits, then dashed through the trees toward the large wooden structure that loomed up ahead.

It *was* The Beast.

It *had* to be The Beast.

What else could it be?

Ashley cried out, "No!" and crumpled to her knees.

"No! No! No!"

It wasn't The Beast.

We were staring at an old barn, half-torn down.

I threw myself down beside Ashley on the grass. For a long time we lay there in gloomy silence, staring up at the blue sky.

We didn't say anything. We didn't need to say anything.

We both knew what we had to do.

We had to get up and go back to the carnival, back to our prison.

What choice did we have?

20

"I want you to see for yourself how brilliant I am," Captain Time boasted. He feverishly worked the controls of his time machine.

Ashley and I stood behind him, watching him work. It had been three days since we made our trip through the park in search of The Beast.

The Captain had been furious with us. But he had forgiven us once again. This morning he had pulled us out of the second show to watch him bring someone else back from the future.

I felt a little excited.

Maybe he would bring someone we knew. Maybe someone with *food!*

By now I was starved. All I could think of was hot dogs and root beer and ice cream and popcorn balls and candy apples.

Even Ashley was beginning to miss food. The night before, we were so hungry, we actually ate the peanuts the kids in the audience threw at us.

Talk about desperate! I figure that's about as low as you can get.

That's how bad things were getting.

"Ah-hah!" the Captain cried as the machine began to shake and shudder and glow bright red. "Let's see who the lucky person from the future is today!"

We watched as the capsule began to rock heavily from side to side, thumping and grinding against the floor.

"Wha—What's happening?" Ashley asked uneasily, beginning to back away.

The machine rocked violently now, back and forth, slamming hard against the floor.

Something very big and very strong was working its way out.

"What's wrong?" I shouted over the pounding racket.

Captain Time cleared his throat nervously.

"No problem, I'm sure," he explained. "Don't be so fearful, children."

The rocking stopped. The machine fell completely still.

The three of us waited and watched in silence, but nothing happened.

The Captain seemed relieved. "See? I told you. No problem. Now, stand away."

With a grand sweep of one arm, he waved us back. With the other he reached out and opened the hatch.

A long black beak jutted out from the time machine.

The beak swung hard. It caught the Captain on the side of the head. Pecked him in the temple. I could see a bloody gash on the Captain's forehead.

The Captain staggered back and fell sprawling to the ground. He didn't move.

With a fierce cry a great black reptile head rose from the time machine. Its jaws opened wide. The jaws were lined with razor-sharp teeth.

Enormous black claws scrabbled at the sides as it struggled to get out.

It pulled free one vast black leathery wing,

then another. It looked as if it were hatching from the huge metal egg of the capsule.

For a few moments it perched on the top of the capsule, staring down at the stunned captain. Then it opened its long beak in a deafening shriek.

Ashley screamed. "James! It's a pterodactyl!"

The creature turned its glowing green eyes in our direction. Letting out another fearful screech, it flapped its great black wings once.

With a loud snap of its jaws, it hopped to the floor. Its neck shot forward as it moved toward us.

"Run, James!" Ashley shouted.

I couldn't move.

Ashley shook me. "Run!" she screamed right into my ear before she herself ran for cover. "Run for your life!"

But I couldn't move. I was frozen in fear.

I stared in horror as the fierce prehistoric creature flapped toward me, snapping its deadly teeth.

21

Finally I forced myself to move.

I backed up, glancing around frantically for something to defend myself with.

A wooden chair! I picked it up. I lifted it over my head—and heaved it at the pterodactyl.

The monster caught it in one claw. Its yellow-green eyes examined the chair with curiosity.

Meanwhile, I examined its talons.

Each one was the size of a carving knife.

I swallowed hard. I had a bitter taste in my mouth as I imagined those claws digging into my skin.

It snapped its beak over the chair, crushing

it. With a horrible crunching sound, it instantly reduced the chair to kindling. When it had finished chewing it up, it tossed aside the last few splinters and returned its attention to me.

A faint moan rose up from the floor.

The Captain sat up, holding his head. When he saw the monster, he let out a strangled cry. "No!"

I watched in horror as the pterodactyl heaved itself into the air. Its leathery wings flapped hard, blasting me with cold, foul-smelling gusts of wind.

There it remained, hovering overhead, fanning me. I backed against the wall and waited for the worst to happen.

But its green eyes weren't on me. They were fixed hungrily on the Captain.

The Captain cried out in fear as the monster swooped down. It pronged him in its razor talons, lifting him high.

"Help me!" the Captain screamed, legs kicking, arms flailing in midair. "Help me—please!"

`Ashley leaped high and tried to grab one of the Captain's legs as he kicked helplessly six feet above the ground.

I leaped, too. I grabbed hold of the Captain's

shoe. Ashley grabbed on to me. Together we hung on and tried to drag him back to the floor.

Overhead, the monster's massive leathery wings beat, kicking up dust from the floor, making a harsh whooshing sound. The three of us were playing tug-of-war.

And the Captain was the rope.

At last our team fell into a heap, with the Captain crashing down on top of us.

"Thank you," he gasped. "Thank you both!"

But we weren't out of danger yet.

The creature circled above us, shrieking.

"Come on!" I shouted, yanking Ashley to her feet. "We've got to run for cover!"

"This way!" the Captain shouted, scrambling to his feet.

The Captain led us away from the time machine, toward the rooms, toward shelter from the shrieking monster. But the Captain was running too fast for us to keep up.

The monster was gaining on us. I felt its shadow, heavy and cold, sweep over us.

The dark shadow lengthened overhead as the bird swooped low.

Our feet pounded the concrete floor. I never

ran so fast in my life. But the ground suddenly gave way. My legs were treading air.

The monster snared us both, one in each claw.

It hooked its long, sharp talons into the fabric of our suits.

Up, up into the air it hoisted us like a pair of helpless mice.

22

Ashley and I wriggled and thrashed as the creature carried us up toward the high ceiling.

Back and forth it flew. It seemed to be searching for something.

For its nest?

Or maybe a nice craggy cliff to set us down on and tear us apart with its razor-sharp beak.

I waited until the creature soared back down toward the floor. Then I reached over and struggled to pull Ashley's silver suit loose from the talons.

I watched as she fell to the ground with a long scream.

Then I did the same for myself, reaching awkwardly back to work myself loose from the monster's grip.

I heard the sound of fabric tearing. Then I fell and landed with a hard thud.

I gasped painfully for air. The wind was knocked out of me.

An unearthly shriek pierced the air. I jerked my head toward the ceiling in terror.

The monster was circling overhead like a giant black vulture, waiting to pick our bones clean.

It swooped closer and closer, snapping its beak like a set of giant, deadly pincers.

Ashley and I cowered in its shadow.

The green eyes narrowed at us greedily. It seemed to be waiting for the right moment.

It opened and closed its beak rapidly, making a nasty clacking sound.

Ashley covered her mouth.

My stomach lurched. My heart pounded.

The monster's breath smelled sour, like rotten meat.

I covered my head with both arms in a feeble attempt to protect myself. But I knew it was useless.

The monster swooped low, coming to eat us alive.

23

Then the great bird let out a startled cry.

But despite its struggles, it flew back. Back. To my shock, it was being pulled to the time machine. It flapped and squawked. But it appeared helpless.

The door of the capsule flew open. The monster struggled as the machine sucked it in. Its talons gripped the rim of the open hatch.

Its wings beat madly, struggling against the force of time itself.

But the creature fought a losing battle. Great hunks of the beast were ripped off and sucked into the machine.

The left wing tore free and disappeared, pulled into the time machine.

Ashley howled and clapped her hand over her mouth.

I held my breath, gaping in amazement.

Seconds later the pterodactyl had disappeared. Torn to pieces. Sucked back into time.

I ran to the machine, my entire body trembling.

Ashley and I waited a minute, then got up and ran over to the time machine.

I peered inside. Empty.

Faint wisps of steam rose from the machine. It smelled like roast turkey.

Captain Time appeared, shaken and dazed. He staggered to the time machine and started to examine it.

"We saved your life," Ashley told him, tugging his sleeve. "Now send us back home."

He ignored her.

"Yes. Send us home!" I insisted.

Finally he stepped back and scratched his head. "I can't," he said softly. "The machine is broken. You're stuck here forever."

24

Much later that night I sprawled on the dusty couch in the Princess's little room.

I was digesting. It was hard work.

I had actually managed to clean my plate at dinner.

Being chased by a pterodactyl can give you an appetite.

"What are we going to do?" Ashley whispered. "How can we escape?"

Before I could answer, I heard voices just outside the little room.

I got up and sneaked over to the door. Holding my breath, I listened.

"You've got to get rid of those kids, Captain," a man's voice was saying.

"You think I don't already know that?" the Captain replied.

"I don't care what you have to do, just do it. The authorities came around today."

"Authorities?" the Captain repeated.

"Don't play dumb with me. The child labor people. They were nosing around the carnival today, asking a lot of questions. Those two kids who escaped the other day? They were running around the fairgrounds, free as you please, causing quite a stir."

"That won't happen again," the Captain said.

"You're right. It won't happen again, because you're going to get rid of them."

"How?" the Captain asked.

"Do whatever you have to do. You're the brilliant scientist. Just make sure that none of them are around here by tomorrow."

"Ashley—did you hear that?" I whispered.

The terrified expression on her face told me that she had heard every word.

"James, we've got to get away from here. We have to go anywhere as quickly as we can!"

"Right. But we need a plan," I told her.

She threw up her hands. "I don't care about a plan. I just wish we had something to wear other than these stupid, stinking silver suits!"

I stared hard at my cousin. "What did you just say?" I demanded.

She eyed me as if I'd just gone nuts. "I said, *stupid, stinking silver suits.*"

"That's it!" I exploded.

"What's it?" She cast me a worried look.
"Our clothes!"

"James, you're not making any sense."

"I'm making plenty of sense!" I shouted, then quickly lowered my voice to an excited whisper. "In fact, I'm making brilliant sense."

Patiently, I explained to her my brainstorm. "Ashley, don't you get it? I understand everything now. The Captain's been lying to us. He brought that dinosaur from the past into the future."

"So?" She stared at me, still baffled.

"So, he can send *us* to the future. He knows how to do it. And now I think *I do, too!*"

26

Ashley peered out between the curtains to make sure no one was lurking out there in the dark, listening to us.

She turned back to me and nodded. "Okay, James. How?"

"Try to remember," I began, "back to when you first climbed out of the time capsule."

Ashley nodded, then blushed. "He made me change right away, into this stupid silver suit," she said. "How could I forget?"

"Exactly!" I exclaimed. "Same with me. At first I thought it was just because he wanted us in a uniform."

She nodded eagerly, following my every word with wide blue eyes.

"But now I think it's because the clothes we arrived in were the clothes of the future. The clothes we changed into, even though they look futuristic, are really clothes from the twenties, made out of fabric and thread from this time."

"James," she said impatiently. "Is this going to start making sense soon? I think I'm losing hope."

"Hang on," I told her. "In one of the time-travel books I read, the woman couldn't travel back to the previous century unless she was wearing an actual dress from that century. So, if we put our own clothes back on—our clothes from the future—we'll create a time warp. And our clothes will take us back to our own time."

Ashley grinned. "I think I get it. Pretty neat!" she cried.

I was really excited now. "When the Captain took away my shorts and shirt and sneakers, he kept mumbling something to himself. 'No traces! No traces!' he said. You see, that meant he didn't want any trace of the 1990s in sight. Because he knew those clothes could take us back to the 1990s."

"You mean," Ashley asked, "all we have to do is put on our real clothes—and we can go home? It sounds a little too simple to me."

"I can't guarantee anything," I replied. "But sometimes the answer is simple." At least I hoped so.

It was our last hope.

Ashley led the way down the hall. "The Captain will be back from dinner any time now," she whispered. "It's now or never, James."

"You're right," I agreed.

No one was in sight—except for a single guard. He sat in the big room, reading the funny papers and chuckling to himself. We got down on our hands and knees and crawled past him until we were out of his sight. Then we leaped to our feet and ran past the time machine.

I hurried to the clothes closet and tugged on the handle.

Locked.

I had forgotten, the Captain always kept it locked. The key was on a big ring he kept in his coat pocket.

We were out of luck.

I examined the door. It was pretty flimsily

made. The Captain's wooden club was hanging on a hook by the door.

I grabbed it and began to bash at the lock until the door splintered and gave way.

Ashley kept an anxious watch. "Hurry, James," she whispered. "Let's get our clothes and get out of here."

Finally the lock fell off. I swung the door open and searched frantically inside.

The closet was empty.

27

We were sunk. That was our last hope.

Ashley threw her hands up in despair. "Our clothes, James!" she wailed. "Where have they taken our clothes?"

"Wait a minute!" I exclaimed. I ran my fingers over the floor. In the back I found a square panel. On one side of the square was a small metal ring.

A trapdoor!

I pried up the ring and tugged it. Nothing happened.

I braced my foot against the closet sill and tugged harder.

The door opened. The false bottom of the closet came up.

And there were our clothes, lying in a jumbled pile. Our wonderful modern clothes.

I'd never been so happy to see a maroon-and-white striped soccer jersey in my life. And my lights! My great new sneakers with the lights in the soles!

Ashley started to undo the hooks of her silver jumpsuit right then and there. I stopped her.

"Not here. Someone might come in and catch us. Let's take our clothes back to the little room. We can change there more safely," I suggested.

Reluctantly she agreed.

Together, we hurried back to the room, our clothes clutched to our chests.

There, with our backs turned to each other, we tore off the silver suits and climbed back into our own clothes.

When we turned around and faced each other, huge grins spread across our faces.

Ashley was wearing her shiny pink clogs, a pair of white Bermuda shorts, and a pale pink halter. The outfit was a little wrinkled, but it looked great to me.

We stood a moment longer in nervous silence, waiting for the time warp to take effect.

I shook my hands out, as if that might speed up our return to the future.

Ashley stamped her clogs.

My heart was beating a mile a minute. My mouth was dry.

We waited to be swept away from the 1930s.

And waited.

Then we gave up and sank down heavily onto the couch.

"Nice try, James." Ashley sighed. "But it didn't work."

"Wait!" I cried. "I have another idea!"

But the door burst open and the Captain barged in.

He took one look at us in our own clothes and his eyes narrowed to angry slits. "Just what do you two think you're doing?" he growled.

He grabbed us, one in each hand. "You two are coming with me," he snarled.

"Where are you taking us?" Ashley choked out.

"Where you've wanted to go all along," he replied, dragging us away.

As if sensing our fears, the Captain stopped in the hallway and turned to Ashley. "You will make a pretty frog-girl, Princess."

Then he spun around to me, jabbing me hard in the chest with his index finger. "Isn't that right, salamander-boy?" he declared.

28

Without another word Captain Time dragged us down the hall.

Where was he taking us? To the big fish tank?

No. He pulled us to the time machine.

"Get in," he commanded.

"Where are you sending us?" I squeaked.

"Back into the past with your friend the pterodactyl. No doubt you'll make delicious bird food."

He shoved us inside and leaned in, turning knobs and flipping levers. "Good riddance to future rubbish," he said. Then he slammed the hatch behind us.

The machine started vibrating.

"James!" Ashley whimpered. "I'm scared. I don't want to go back to the time of dinosaurs!"

I was so frightened, my teeth were chattering. But I managed to turn the knobs and flip the levers to the exact opposite settings.

Captain Time may have wanted us to go backward. But *forward* was where we were headed, if I had any say.

I waited. I was so nervous I wanted to scream.

'I had myself a real case of the screamies.

The screamies.

"I've got it!" I exclaimed.

Ashley looked even more scared than before. "What are you talking about now, James?"

I reached into the back pocket of my shorts. They were mashed nearly flat, but they were still there! My pack of Karamel Krecmies.

"Only two left," I murmured. "Just enough."

"Enough for what?" Ashley demanded.

I handed her a Karamel Kreemie. "Just put it in your mouth and chew it, Ashley," I told her.

She shook her head and pointed at her teeth. "You keep forgetting. My braces!"

I couldn't believe her. "Ashley, don't be a jerk. Chew it anyway. So what if it sticks to your teeth? It will save you from being dinosaur food!"

She stared at me, not understanding.

I turned to her and tried to explain. "The candy from the 1990s will create a time warp. I understand completely now. We have to have something from the future outside us *and* inside us! We're already wearing our 1990s clothes. Now we need to chew the 1990s candy. And it will take us back to our time."

The machine was shaking now, rocking back and forth.

"I hope you're right," Ashley said. She stared at the candy in her hand.

"Just eat it!" I shouted at her over the mounting roar of the time machine.

I was already chewing my piece.

The sticky sweetness filled my mouth and slid down my throat like syrup.

Would it work? Was my idea right?

Would the candy and the clothes carry us forward in time?

I stared at the capsule walls. They began vibrating with a high-pitched hum. The walls started to fade, and a strange yellow light spread over us.

"Ashley, look! I'm starting to fade!" I cried.

Ashley's body remained solid. Why wasn't she fading along with me?

As the time machine walls faded away, a furious Captain Time came into view. "How dare you reverse the controls!" he screamed.

His voice exploded inside my head.

He reached forward and grabbed Ashley's arm. "You're staying here with me, Princess!"

Inch by inch Captain Time pulled her out of the capsule—back into his time!

I was fading, fading away. Why wasn't Ashley fading with me?

And then I realized what the problem was.

The candy. The Karamel Kreemie. She still hadn't eaten the Karamel Kreemie.

"Chew the Kreemie!" I screamed at her. "Chew it or you'll be left behind!"

"It's too late!" Ashley wailed. "Too late!" She uttered a sob. And then in a trembling voice she called, "Bye, James."

"The candy!" I cried, feeling far away from her.

I saw her stuff it into her mouth. I saw her bite down hard on it.

And as she bit down, the Captain began to grow smaller and smaller. We were leaving him behind.

"Chew it!" I shouted. "Keep chewing!"

We were rushing forward now, through people and cities, through time itself. Every cell in my body was tingling, as blurred faces and buildings and strange places flashed past me.

My skin was on fire.

"Keep chewing!" I shouted to Ashley. "It's got to work! It's got to."

My stomach was in my throat. Bright lights and colors exploded around me. I was falling through the air. Faster and faster, the wind whizzing past me at a dizzying rate.

Suddenly I felt smooth cold metal beneath my hands. I opened my eyes and looked down.

I was holding on to a metal bar.

A metal safety bar.

I was on The Beast!

Ashley and I were roaring down that last hill. Behind me, I heard the screams of the other riders. The bright lights of the amusement park sparkled and winked and twirled around me.

The sky was purple. The orange moon was shining overhead.

Not quite full.

We had done it. We had returned to our own space and time. My jaws ached from all that chewing.

"We did it, James!" Ashley cried happily.

The Beast slowed down and clattered into the platform.

I climbed out and nearly dropped to my knees to kiss that cold, beautiful concrete I thought I'd never see again.

But what time was it? What day? We'd been gone for days.

"Look, James!" Ashley pointed up.

The sky exploded in a shower of fireworks, sparkling bursts of orange and blue and pink and purple.

"It's still Wednesday, James! The same day we left!"

"How can you tell?" I asked as a great white rocket spiraled high into the air and exploded in a cascade of sparkles.

"Don't you remember? The fireworks!" she

cried joyfully. "That's why we came to the park today. Because we wanted to see the fireworks."

I nodded, still in shock. Then I remembered.

There was going to be a fireworks display tonight, half an hour before closing time.

"You know what that means, James?" my cousin asked, her blue eyes flashing.

"No. What?" I asked.

"It means we have time to ride The Beast again!"

She grabbed my arm and dragged me back onto the platform. "Let's go. One more time!"

ABOUT THE AUTHOR

"Where do you get your ideas?"

That's the question that R. L. Stine is asked most often. "I don't know where my ideas come from," he says. "But I do know that I have a lot more scary stories in my mind that I can't wait to write."

So far, he has written nearly three dozen mysteries and thrillers for young people, all of them best-sellers.

Bob grew up in Columbus, Ohio. Today he lives in an apartment near Central Park in New York City with his wife, Jane, and fourteen-year-old son, Matt.

THEY'LL HAUNT YOU FOREVER

**Do you believe in ghosts?
Don't say no until you read
THE GHOSTS OF FEAR STREET—
a spooky new series created by R. L. Stine.**

R. L. STINE'S GHOSTS OF FEAR STREET #1

HIDE AND SHRIEK

Coming in July, 1995

Randy Clay is surprised how fast she makes friends when she transfers to Shadyside Middle School. Being the new kid isn't bad at all.

Until her new friends tell her the legend of the Fear Street Woods. . . .

Every year, on the twelfth of June, all the twelve-year-olds in Shadyside get to play a game of hide-and-seek. With a ghost named Pete.

Pete's been dead for many, many years. And he wants a new body. Whomever he tags during the game has to give him one.

Randy is terrified when she hears that Pete likes the new kids the best.

If Pete tags Randy, she won't be the newest kid in school anymore.

She'll be the newest ghost on Fear Street!

R. L. STINE'S GHOSTS OF FEAR STREET #2

WHO'S BEEN SLEEPING IN MY GRAVE?

Coming in September, 1995

Anybody can scare Zack Pepper. Anybody. Say "boo" and he jumps ten feet in the air.

Zack is determined to change all that. He buys a book called POWER KIDS. And promises himself he'll never allow anyone to scare him again.

But how can he keep his promise when he finds out the truth about his substitute teacher, Miss Gaunt?

Miss Gaunt's a ghost! And she's planning to give a special student private lessons—in her grave in the Fear Street Cemetery.

Pete and Miss Gaunt are only two of the ghosts of Fear Street. There are many others. Each with a story to tell.

And they are all dying to meet you!

YOU COULD WIN A CHANCE TO RIDE
THE BEAST®

A MINSTREL BOOK   *Paramount Parks*   UNITED AIRLINES

One First Prize: Trip for three to Paramount's Kings Island (home of the BEAST®) or the Paramount theme park of the winner's choice.

Four Second Prizes: Four Single-Day Admission Tickets to the Paramount Park near you.

Twenty-Five Third Prizes: An autographed copy of *The Beast 2*

Name_____Birthdate_____

Address_____

City_____State___Zip_____

Phone (   )_____

POCKET BOOKS *Win a Chance to Ride The Beast*® SWEEPSTAKES Official Rules:

NOW THAT YOU'VE READ A THRILLER, RIDE A THRILLER.

Bruce Coville's Alien Adventures

What happens when a tiny spaceship crashes through Rod Allbright's window and drops a crew of superpowerful aliens into the middle of his school project? Rod is drafted by Captain Grakker to help the aliens catch a dangerous interstellar criminal—in a chase that takes them all over the galaxy!

ALIENS ATE MY HOMEWORK

I LEFT MY SNEAKERS IN DIMENSION X

AND COMING SOON...

THE SEARCH FOR SNOUT

by BRUCE COVILLE

A MINSTREL® BOOK

Published by Pocket Books

1043-02

The Midnight Society has a scary
new story to tell. . .

A brand new thriller series based on the hit
Nickelodeon® show!

THE TALE OF THE
SINISTER STATUES
by **John Peel**

THE TALE OF
CUTTER'S TREASURE
by **David L. Seidman**

A new title every other month!!

🐎 A MINSTREL® BOOK

Published by Pocket Books

1053-02